THE UGLY DUCKLING

By Hans Christian Andersen
Adapted by Ben Cruise
Illustrated by Lisa McCue

A GOLDEN BOOK • NEW YORK
Western Publishing Company, Inc., Racine, Wisconsin 53404

One fine summer day a mother duck's eggs began to crack. Six little ducklings sprang from their shells. "Peep, peep," they cried.

"Are you all here?" the mother asked. She counted the ducklings. Then she looked into the nest. The largest egg was still unhatched.

The mother duck sat and sat, and at last the big egg began to crack. "Peep, peep," cried the new duckling.

The mother gasped when she saw him, for he was big and ugly. "He does not look like the others," she thought. "I wonder if he can swim."

The ducklings splashed into the water, with the strange ugly duckling last of all. He swam merrily with the rest.

The mother was pleased. After a long swim, she marched her children into the barnyard to meet the other birds.

"Look at that big ugly one!" some ducks murmured. They began to laugh and peck at him.

"Leave him alone!" cried the mother. "He swims well, and he will grow to be a fine drake, I am sure!"

But, day after day, the poor duckling's life in the barnyard grew worse. Not only did the ducks make fun of him, but the chickens and turkeys did as well. Finally he could stand no more teasing, and he ran away.

He soon came to a swamp that was surrounded by woods.
There he slept all night under a friendly moon.

In the morning the wild swamp ducks found him. "You
certainly are ugly," one wild duck said. "But you may stay here
as long as you don't bother us."

So the duckling stayed alone in the rushes for two whole days. Then two wild geese came by, wanting to pass the time.

"You are so ugly that I like you," one of them said. "Come with us, and we will introduce you to some other geese."

But, before they could go, a great *bang, bang* rang through the woods. In a flash, the two wild geese were gone.

Hunters and their dogs were coming through the woods.

The duckling looked about him. Close by, he saw an enormous dog. Its tongue hung out of its mouth.

The dog came closer and closer. But, after a good look at the ugly duckling, it ran off another way.

"Thank goodness!" the ugly duckling cried.

When he was sure it was quite safe, the ugly duckling started to fly away. Flying was difficult, for there was a strong wind. But he kept on till evening, when he came to a little tumbledown cottage.

The duckling slipped inside. The cottage belonged to an old
woman who lived there with a tomcat and a hen.

"What good luck!" said the old woman when she saw the
ugly duckling. "We shall have duck's eggs, if it doesn't turn out
to be a drake."

"Can you lay eggs?" the hen asked the ugly duckling.
"Can you purr or arch your back?" the tomcat asked him.
"No," said the ugly duckling. "I can swim."

"Swim?" said the hen. "What earthly good is swimming?
You should learn to lay eggs."

"Or purr," added the tomcat.

"You do not understand me," said the young drake.
"I had best be on my way."

Outside, the autumn winds were howling. The young drake swam and dived, but he was all alone.

One frosty evening a flock of beautiful big white birds flew past. The young drake felt strange when he saw them. He cried out to them and spun around in the water. But soon the birds were out of sight.

The weather grew colder, and one day the pond froze. The bird was stuck fast in the ice.

Next morning a kind peasant happened by. He broke the ice with his wooden clogs, and then he carried the bird home.

The peasant's children wanted to play with the bird, and they chased him around the room. He flew up in panic and spilled the milk on the floor.

"Oh!" the peasant's wife cried, raising her hands in horror. This frightened the bird still more. He flew into the new butter, and then into the flour bin.

"Out of my house, before you spoil all the food!" the woman cried, and she drove the young drake outdoors again.

For the rest of the winter he slept in the marsh grass.
When the sun began to shine warm again, he awoke. His feathers were a lighter color now. When he stretched his wings, he found that they were big and strong.

The bird flew until he came to a splendid garden. There was a pond, and on it glided three of the beautiful white birds he had seen before.

"They will not let me swim with them," he thought sadly, "but at least I can gaze at them in all their beauty."

The swans swam closer, and the bird bowed his head as they passed. But there, in the water, what did he see...

A graceful, long-necked white bird looked back at him, and this bird was lovelier than all the others. He had been a swan all along, though none had known it. And now all the beautiful swans were gathering about to welcome him.